Mel Bay Presents

How to Sing American

Pronunciation for Jazz, Rock, R&B and other non-classical singers

by Joyce Lucia

CD CONTENTS

1 2 3 4 5 6 7 8 9 0

Visit us on the Web at www.melbay.com — E-mail us at email@melbay.com

How to Sing American

Table of Contents

Part 1
Vowels

Diphthongs

Part II
Consonants

Appendix

How to Sing American

By its very nature **international** in interest, this book teaches foreign (and American) singers how to pronounce lyrics in American English. Its focus is singers with English as a Second Language, since they are the primary audience who wants to learn English pronunciation! (This focus came about because 9 out of 10 people who take Diction at Berklee College of Music are international. Thus I'd suspect that they would be the largest audience for this information.)

Besides learning to pronounce words correctly in American English the student will find his singing actually improves! The classical world knows the importance of Diction — hence classes on correct German, French, Italian.... However, the voices of classical singers need not be the **only** ones to reap benefits from this concept. The use of the International Phonetic Alphabet (IPA) which has catalogued sounds to over 140 world languages, gives the non-classical singer **immediate** improvement.

Teaching vocal classes at Berklee, I see first-hand the need for a study of **casual** English pronunciation as occurs in many popular song lyrics. For example, many R&B songs use the word "gotta" rather than "got to" or "dontcha" in place of "don't you." This is a secondary concern, however, because singers need to **learn to use the IPA first**, before engaging in such subtleties.

English vowels and consonants can be represented by IPA symbols. Once a singer is familiar with the sounds associated with the IPA symbols and can rewrite lyrics using them, he or she can immediately produce American sounds devoid of any local accents (such as those of Boston or New York).

Note that the words "English" and "American" are sometimes used interchangeably in this text. The language described is "English" but its casual use is denoted in the word "American."

Let's assume that most singers have "good ears." Now I'm asking for use of their **brains** in applying an already accepted system of notating sound. This gives the singer **one more aspect** of her voice **that she controls.** (She already had pitch, rhythm, and color... now vowel/consonant choice is part of her mental perception of sound.)

Joyce Lucia

Member, International Phonetic Society and
Teachers of English to Speakers of Other Languages (TESOL)
Associate Professor, Voice Department
Berklee College of Music

I would like to thank several people for their help in the production of this text. First, I would like to thank Jan Shapiro, Chair of the Voice Department at Berklee College of Music. Jan encouraged me to use my teaching at Berklee as well as student and faculty involvement in the development of this book. Her openness and foresight were a foundation upon which many of these ideas developed as I taught the course American Diction.

Tomoko Nagahori and Emily Arbuckle, students, were volunteers for photography of the vowel and consonant mouth positions seen within. My husband was the patient photographer.

And, of course, thanks to the International Phonetic Society and my former diction teachers, whose inspiration over the past 25 years made these pages possible.

How to use this book

This book was originally written to be used in a classroom where singers would prepare song lyrics each week, adding the vowels/consonants they'd learned the previous week. There are several ways in which you can use these ideas.

With a teacher:

This is probably the easiest way.

• You can prepare a song lyric for the material you will sing at your weekly lesson. This gives a good structure to your learning and makes it organized. If your teacher studied music in a conservatory, he or she is aware of English Diction and can help you weekly.

With a friend:

Having another person with the same goal is GREAT.

• You can exchange ideas, sing for one another and even keep track of progress.

By yourself:

• Find a song you want to sing. Then, with the help of this book, write the lyrics on a lined sheet of paper and mark the IPA symbols you are familiar with. Be sure to follow the rules in the text for writing lyrics with IPA page 3.

In just a few days, you should see improvement in your pronunciation AND in your singing voice!

Using a tape recorder:

I think the tape recorder is the best friend a singer could ever have. The recorder will listen and keep an accurate record of your progress.

• Tape a few songs BEFORE you have learned *How To Sing American.* Save this tape, because you should compare it to the way you sing AFTER you have learned to pronounce American easily and naturally. (This is true for American singers too!!!)

While you read this book:

• Each week, record a familiar melody, singing on a single vowel. Begin with [u]. Can you sing the entire melody with "vowel commitment"? That means not changing the vowel sound whether the notes are high, low, fast or slow.

• Try to memorize the IPA symbols for vowels, so that you need not look at the vowel triangle while writing them into your lyrics. At first, however, keep your book open to the Vowel Triangle (page viii).

• If you speak English fluently, you will eventually be able to choose the appropriate vowels without even writing them down.

• Initial focus should be on the long notes at the end of lines. Ballads are a great place to start. Any style.

• Check your choices in a dictionary that uses IPA. (Most dictionaries for non-English speakers use IPA. There are fewer English or American dictionaries that do, but they can be found!) Remember that singers' pronunciation is slightly different from standard dictionaries. See p. 35.

• Tape record yourself singing songs on single vowels, then with American pronunciation. Were there any words that were difficult to understand? Also, you may have someone who doesn't know the song

• Were any difficulties caused by vowels, or was the problem with pronunciation of the consonants?

• Learn all the American consonant sounds. Use the enclosed CD to give you accurate examples. You may stop the CD and copy the sounds after each one is made. This will teach you the sounds more quickly than "singing along" - a popular although inefficient choice of many. "Singing along" will only ensure that you can sing the sounds when the CD is playing!

• Speak the lyrics into the tape recorder. You must be able to say them smoothly, at a tempo faster than you will sing. If you can do this, then singing them should not be a problem. (Remember to tape the melody without any lyrics. Play back the tape to find any musical problems.)

• Sing the lyrics into the tape recorder. You can now check your "finished product" before you share it with the world! Of course, you should listen to American singers to actually learn songs, but YOU now understand the diction YOURSELF!

Symbols used in this book

Several symbols used throughout this book need explanation:

* [ ] is used to surround I.P.A. symbols
* " " surrounds American Spelling of words and individual sounds so as not to confuse them with IPA
* √ represents a breath
* [ɔ] is the symbol singers use to represent both [ɒ] and [ɔ]
* ‿ — a curved arrow marks the elision or connection between two words
* [ʔ] marks the glottal stop occasionally used by American singers
* **"sil manuscript font"** is used throughout the book. It contains IPA symbols used to define singing sounds.

Note: The font is available through the IPA. You can locate information about the International Phonetic Association by searching the World Wide Web.

The IPA Vowel Triangle

There are 9 vowels in English, 2 closed and 7 open. Below, a sample word is listed for each of the phonetic symbols from the International Phonetic Alphabet or IPA:

[i] "he" [u] "who"

[I] "hit" [U] "hood"

[E] "head" [ɜ] [ɔ] "hot"

[æ] "had" [ə] [ʌ] "hug"

[a] "la"

[ə] appears only in unstressed syllables
[æ] similar to the neutral, but appears in stressed syllables
try saying "earth" or "girl" as the Beatles might say them.

THE FIVE DIPHTHONGS:

For singing, we need only 5 diphthongs!

[a:i] "night"
[E:i] "day"
[ɔ:i] "boy"
[a:u] "now"
[ɔ:u] "no"

mē, mā, mah, mō, moo

Vowel Triangle Mouth Positions

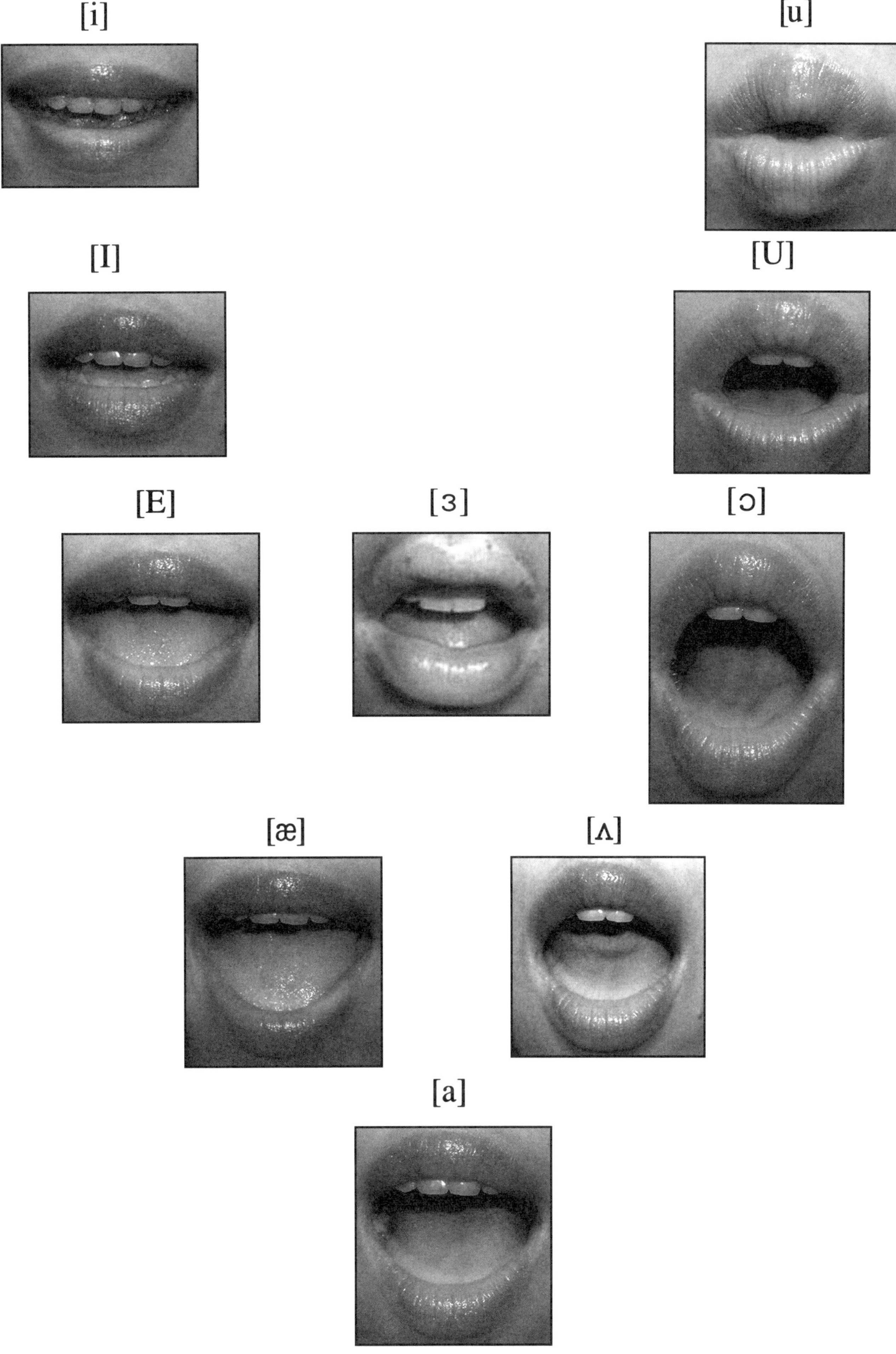

The "R" Pages

Madeleine Marshall, in her classic book *The Singer's Manual of English Diction*[1] has a page entitled "No Bad Social Consequences;" Her suggestion that "R" be sometimes omitted when singing must have sounded preposterous in the mid 1900's. Well it's more than 50 years later, and the concept is still controversial. However, it's logical. Remember that these rules are FOR SINGING ONLY. Here's how they go:

1. When singing a word where "r" is followed by a consonant, you OMIT the "r."

2. When "r" is followed by a pause (the end of a sentence or primarily when "r" is at the end of a word) the "r" is OMITTED.

3. When "r" is followed by a vowel; it STAYS. Yes, that's right; you sing "r" about 1/3 of the time in English.

Why is this the case?

Uvular "R" following a vowel imparts a characteristic which invades or colors the vowel preceding it. This problem is omitted in English classical singing by using rolled "r's," as in the other European languages.

How will people understand the singer who omits
the letter "r"? Won't the words be incomprehensible?

We understand through context, rather than through single words alone. (That's why it is often difficult for one to understand a foreign language when his study has been based on learning single words.) So, when you sing "When you wish upon a stah," the listener imagines the final "r" and hears nothing unusual from the "r-less" singer.

Let's use a sample word for each of the 3 cases above:

1. "start" = "start" **Do not pronounce R before a consonant**

2. "star" = "star" **Do not pronounce R before a pause**

3. "red" = "red" **but, Do pronounce R before a vowel**

"What determines whether "R" is before a pause? What if the next word starts with a vowel?"

Good question! If the next word begins with a vowel, the "r" goes to the RIGHT and elides with the next word.

Example:

"Star‿eyes, pretty little Star‿eyes"

Here the "r" from Star goes RIGHT and elides with the word "eyes." This enables smooth and understandable singing. (To omit the "r" would have caused the singer to make a new attack on the word "eyes," possibly causing a glottal sound, and definitely reducing the legato.)

There are several other conditions which determine how "r's"are sung. Two of them are:

1. Removing silent "E's"
2. Syllabification

---

[1] Madeleine Marshall, *The Singer's Manual of English Diction* © 1946 Schirmer Books, New York

Removing the Silent "E"

In most cases silent "e" will not change the position of neighboring letters, causing a change in their pronunciation. However, when the "e" follows an "r," its removal leaves the "r" before a pause rather than a vowel, causing it to be silent. Example:

"are"

1. First we remove the final "e," leaving "ar~~e~~"
2. Now with "r" before a pause, the "r" becomes silent, making it "a~~re~~" or [a] phonetically

A phrase which incorporates the same idea is :
"Wherever you are"
With the silent e's and "r's" crossed out, it looks like this:

"Whereve~~r~~ you a~~re~~"

Syllabification

Syllabification is a big word, and an important one. The way we divide syllables determines how "smooth" or "legato" our line sounds. Therefore it determines how easily we sing.

In the dictionary, words are divided using several rules: between double consonants; between compound words or between roots and suffixes or prefixes. However, for singing, the dictionary offers us little help in how to sing a word legato. An example is:

"sun - shine"

If we sang using this syllabification, we would have to close the first note on the sound [n]. Rather, the singer should divide syllables after the vowels: su-nshine. Since notes are sustained on vowels, with consonants simply dividing syllables, this is possible.

This concept can be used on single-syllable as well as on multi-syllable words. Let's see how it works for an entire song line primarily with one syllable words and the consonants going RIGHT:

"Y o u w a r e t h e s u - n s h i - n o fm y l i f e..."

[ju wa thə sʌ nʃa:i nʌv ma:i la:if]

This principle is more simply defined as "xo xo xo," with "x" representing a consonant and "o" representing a vowel.
Soon the singer doesn't have to think consciously of this and automatically sings with consonants going to the

RIGHT.

However, whenever one takes a breath following a word, or when there's a punctuation mark which one wishes to emphasize, the final consonant remains on the preceding word and does not go right onto the next.

Example:

"You are the sunshine (breath*) of my life." (*Even though this is not an ideal place to take a breath, one often occurs.) Here the final "n" of "sunshine" remains attached to "sunshine," rather than forming the beginning of the next word.

So the phrase would sound like this:

"You are the sunshine (breath) of my life...."
rather than: "You are the sunshi nof my life..." (no breath within the phrase)

Another example of a consonant not going RIGHT onto the next word would occur when the 1st word was followed by a period or other strong punctuation mark.

"What kind of man is this, an empty cell? A lonely ......"

The final "l" of cell would ordinarily go RIGHT onto "ɑ," but was followed by a "?," so it stays with "cell."

More syllabification

1. When a word begins with a vowel, it usually takes the final consonant of the previous word. Examples:

Fuel ⤻ oil

Bad ⤻ art

Mark these with a curved arrow ⤻ connecting the two words.

2. Mark breaths with checks [√] in your homework, since where you breathe affects whether words are connected or not. (See first syllabification page.)

3. Here are sample lyrics with IPA written above them.

```
 [E:i ]  [ æ ]     [i]  [a:u] [a:i] [u]   [a:i] [ə]  [i]   [ʌ]      [u]
They  asked me  how  I  knew my ca/reer was  through...

 [ɔ:i] [i][æ][ʌ] √ [I]  [æ]     [ɔ]     [ɔ:u]  [ɔ]  [ʌ] [ʌ][æ][ʌ]
Poi/nci/a/na,  is  that  your  nose  or  a ba/na/na?.....
```

How To Write Lyrics For IPA Analysis

In Ink

1. WRITE SONG LYRICS. (IF ON COMPUTER, ONE SPACE BETWEEN EACH LETTER AND 3 SPACES BETWEEN EACH WORD: "Y O U   A R E   T H E   S U N S H I N E   O F   M Y   .....")
2. SKIP A LINE BETWEEN EACH LINE OF WRITING.

In Pencil

3. CROSS OUT SILENT "E'S" AND SILENT "R'S"
*remember that only "r" before a vowel is pronounced. All others are not.
4. SYLLABIFY EACH WORD.
5. FINALLY, ADD IPA SYMBOLS ABOVE APPROPRIATE SYLLABLES. THE IPA IS WRITTEN IN SQUARE BRACKETS [ ].

VOWELS

Vowels

[u]

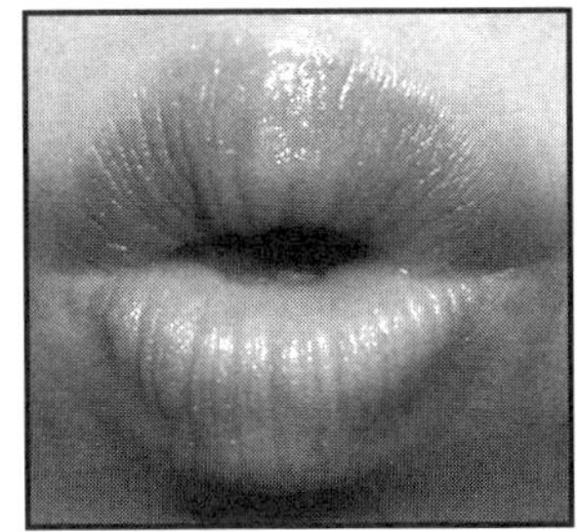

One of the two "closed" vowels in English, [u] can be formed by slight puckering and forward projection of the lips. Some American words that contain [u] are:

1. The **goon** under the **June moon** at **noon**
2. It's **cool** not to **drool** like a **fool**, even in a **pool**.*

*Be careful not to make [u] words that end in "l" sound as if they were two syllables! (example: tool; cool)

3. The **boot** goes with the **suit** that cost lots of **loot**. What a **hoot!**
4. **Mu**sic can be **beau**tiful but **few jew**els ride a **mule**.
5. **Blue** is a color. **Brew** is beer. **Few** means not too many. "**Boo**" makes you fear.
6. Through **you**, on the way to the **zoo**, I get the **clue**, it's in my **shoe**.
7. A **poor**, **foo**lish **lure** is something **sure to you.**
8. **School** days, **school** days are they Golden **Rule** days?

Some [u] words from song lyrics:

1. ...what **you do to** me; it's so **new** to me; what **you do to** me.
2. **...blue moon...swoon...June**
3. **...you** and I, love forever **true**
4. **...ooo**, what did I **do**? What did I **do to you**?
5. Don't be **cruel** to a heart that's **true**.
6. Only **you**...**who**...we're **through**...
7. **Foo**lish little girl...he wanted **you**...**you** can **do**.
8. **Beau**tiful love...for **beau**ty...come **true**.
9. Don't be **rude** when I'm in the **mood**.
10. Hey **Jude**, don't be a **fool**.

[i]

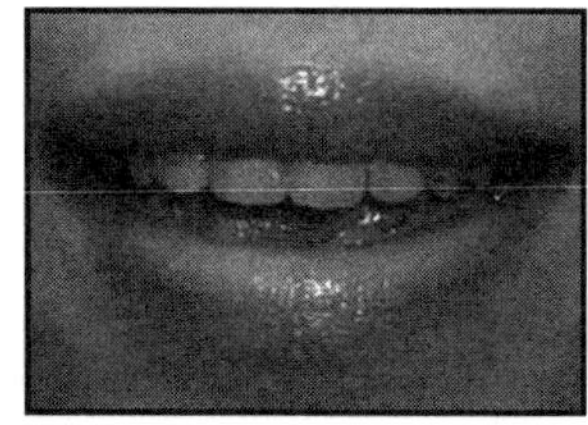

To create the American sound [i] the sides of your lips pull back, teeth show slightly and your cheeks puff up. (Don't try to keep your mouth in an [u] shape!)

Sing these words with [i]:

1. be beat bean beef bead beam beep beer beak
2. deep deal deed deem Dean dear **di**va
3. fee feet feed feel **fe**male fear feast
4. he heel heed hear he's
5. key keep keen eek
6. Lee lead leaf leak lean leap lease leave
7. me meek meal mean meat meet
8. need kneel neap near niece neat knees
9. peace peek peel peep peer Pete peeve
10. ski sneeze speed see seat sweet seep seed
11. **v**-neck veal **V**enus veep veer

Some song lyrics with [i]

1. When a **bee** lies **sleeping**, it **seems sweet** as a **dream**
2. **Be** true to me. **Free** again, luck**y** **me**
3. **Please please me** like I **please** you
4. **Dream**, I **dream** of you. You **seem** to **be real**.
5. Should **we**? I a**gree** it's **three**.
6. **These three things** I ask of **thee**
7. **Baby**, I'm half craz**y**, cuz you'd look **sweet** upon the **seat**....
8. You give **me** fever. It's **Bea**ver **Clea**ver the de**cei**ver.
9. **Dream Wea**ver, I be**lieve** I wouldn't **leave** her.

[ɔ] in song lyrics:

Sing each example below.
1. on a single note melody,
2. on any melody of your choice.

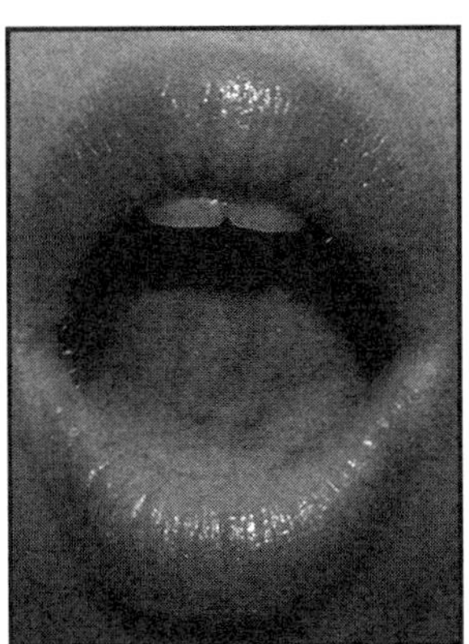

1. Be**cause** of you there's a **song**; that's not **wrong**.
2. **God not dog; dog not hot-dog.**
3. It's **on**; it's **off**; you laugh; you **cough**.
4. I've **got** you; **caught** you; **fought** you; **bought** you.
5. A **fog**gy night a **jogging** **hog**.
6. So **lock** the door; **stock** the shelves
7. **Prom** time, CD **rom** time; maybe even **Mom** time.
8. It's **awe**some. Study **law** some.

Words with the sound [ʌ]

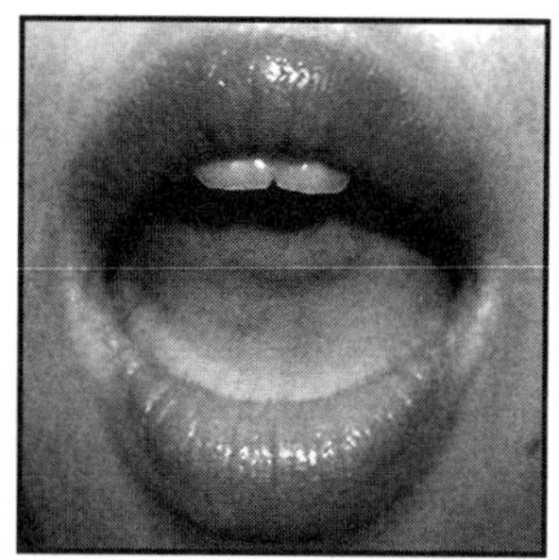

* Bold print syllables indicate desired vowel sound in that word

1. love dove **above**
2. mug rug bug hug lug jug dug pug
3. but nut gut rut cut hut mutt putt what
4. come gum dumb hum numb rum some sum
5. jump lump bump dump hump pump rump
6. fudge judge nudge **pudg**y
7. just buts dust gust lust must rust
8. buzz ‘cuz does fuzz was
9. lung hung stung rung
10. drunk funk junk monk punk sunk skunk
11. enough rough tough stuff cuff puff

[ʌ] in song lyrics

I **love** you; you were sent **from** a**bove**

And we’ll have **fun, fun, fun.....**

My little runaway, **run, run, run, run.**

Someday I’ll find my **love.**

I live for the **sun** because it means **fun**.

Falling in **love** is **won**derful, it’s **won**derful.

We’ve only **just** be**gun**, now that we’re **one**.

Make of our hearts **one** heart.

Hey **bro**ther, where’s your **mo**ther?

If it’s not **one** thing, it’s a**no**ther.

Run for **co**ver.

The sound [ɜ]

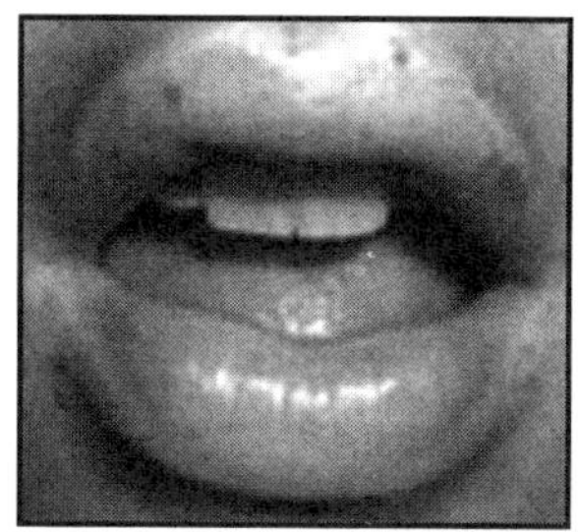

[ɜ] is always followed by the letter "r" which isn't pronounced! This is the sound in the word "girl" when pronounced by the Beatles (British). Listen to their album *Rubber Soul* for the song "Girl" or to "You're Gonna Lose that Girl." You may also listen to British pronunciation and to the CD *American English Sounds.*

[ɜ] is found in stressed syllables only. When this sound appears in unstressed syllables, it appears as [ə] such as in the words "mother" [mʌ ðə] or "father" [faðə]

Some words with [ɜ] to sing:
1. On a single note each
2. On 2 notes each
3. On 3 notes each, etc.

girl	first	fir	flirt
bird	earth	world	curl
birth	third	furs	dirt

Sing these lines that contain words in **bold** print that use the sound [ɜ]. Be sure to sing the **bold** words **slowly**, thinking about the vowel sound. Make a tape recording as you do this. Listen to the tape. How did you do?

Girl, girl you put me in a **whirl**.

I'm the most beautiful **girl** in the **world**.

The first time ever I saw your **skirt**.

I **heard** it from the **worst per**son.

He came in **third**.

Happy **birth**day to you. Happy **birth**day to you.

It's your **birth**day. It's my **birth**day too, yeah.

Fire can **burn** you.

What's that **worth**?

Samuel Barber wrote the "**Her**mit Songs."

Words with [I]

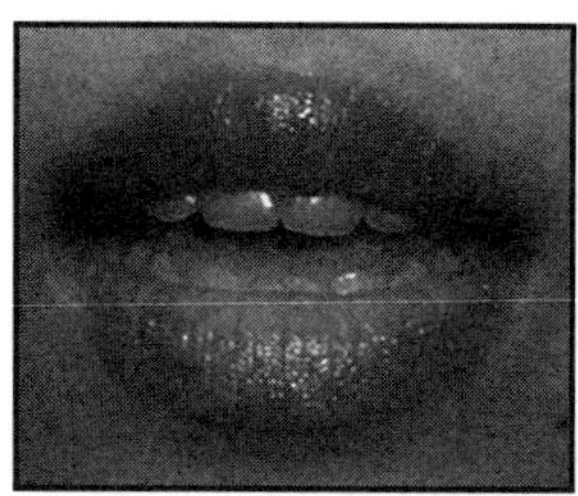

[I] called "open I" exists in English, German, and Italian. For speakers of languages such as Spanish and Japanese, which do not contain [I], listen carefully to the enclosed CD and to American singers when they sing this sound, because [I] may be difficult to discern from [i].

Fish gotta **swim** and **pigs** gotta fly.

Win and they'll **give it** to you.

I love **him**, he's my **Bill**.

She **will** do **it** now.

Little kid in "show **biz**."

Let's compare [i] and [I]

[i]	[I]
bean	bin
deep	dip
feel	fill
green	grin
heap	hip
leap	lip
meek	Mick
meal	mill
peek	pick
reap	rip
seat	sit
teak	tick
weak	wick

You can learn to make this sound by imitating American pronunciation on the CD.

[E]

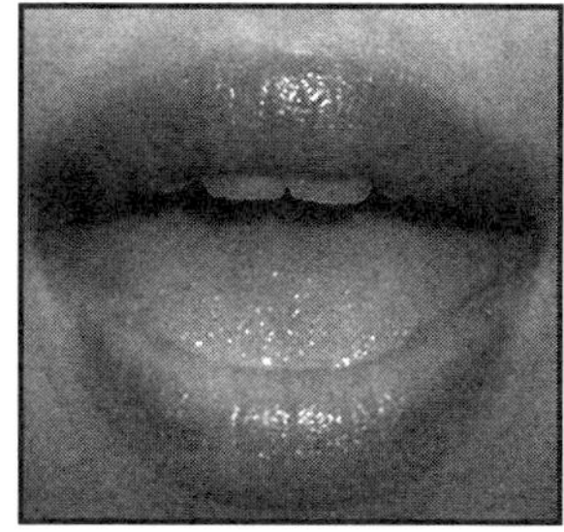

a **men**	a **gain**	pre **tend**	re **me** mber
men	**Se pte** mber	De **ce** mber	No **ve** mber
then	**wea** ther	**whe** ther	**ne** ver
when	**whe ne** ver	**whe re** ver	**we** dding
get	to **ge** ther	fo **re** ver	**pe** bble
let	**be** tter	bled	bell
met	**me** thod	**ble** ssed	**hea** ven
pet	friends	**re** la tive	**me** lo dy
web	**ye** ster day	fell	**se** cond
felt	less	west	guest
help	**ve** ry	**Ste** lla	**jea** lous

Words with [U]

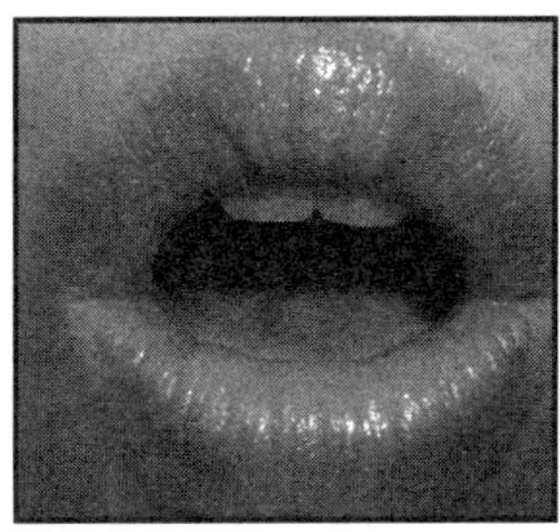

You're too **good** to be true.

I'm not made of **wood**.

I **should** care. I **should** go without sleeping.

It's **full** of water.

Mom got me a **cookbook**.

Put one **foot** behind the other one.

I **could** have danced all night.

I **could** write a **book** about the way you **look**.

Look, it's the **crook's book**.

[æ]

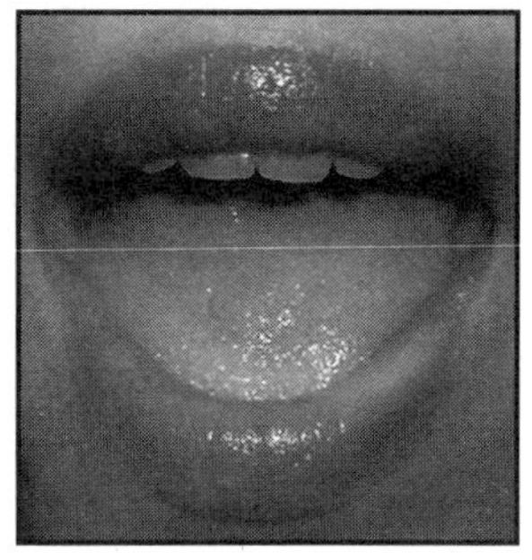

ma tter	dad	fad	glad	sad
ha bit	grab	cab	dab	lab
lack	jack	sax	sack	tack
laugh	**ta** ffy	draft	**a** fter	half
bag	fat	cat	sash	nag
back	lack	**pa** tter	pack	tack
ba llet	**ba** llot	**ca** llous	**da** lly	hat
ban	can	fan	man	cash
ba ptize	cap	gap	**ha** ppen	map
ma rry	**fa** shion	**ta** rry	**pa** ssion	**ca** rry

***This sound is seldom, if at all, used in classical English.**
I think of [æ] as a distinctly American sound.

[a]

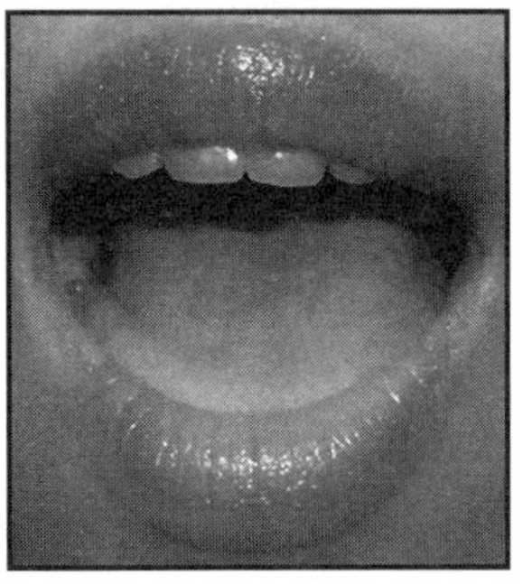

Words with [a] such **as "la"**

haha	heart	star	park
fa	start	car	hark
la	cart	far	card
ma	dart	bar	scarf
pa	far	mark	started

[ə]

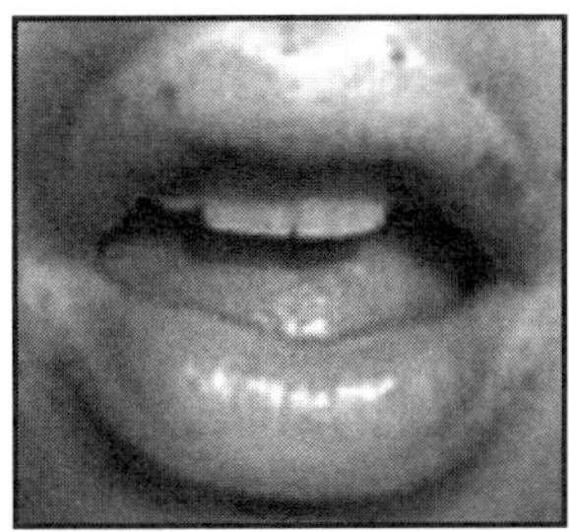

This sound is called a "neutral." In French it is called a "mute"; in German it's name is "schwa." Appearing only in unstressed syllables, it sounds like [ɜ]

mo ther	o ther	nei ther
bro ther	su mmer	wi nter

<u>Experiment:</u> try singing the words above, substituting every other possible vowel sound but [ə]. Is there another one which you can sustain in <u>all the words?</u>

At first, this sound may be more difficult to learn than the others, but it is important, <u>because it is always used when no other IPA sound fits!</u>

Unfortunately singers, unlike speakers, are sometimes forced to sustain this vowel sound because songwriters have it set on a quarter note or greater.

Think of the Latin song "Roses and Roses." The 2nd syllable of "roses" is sometimes sustained for more than a half note! For this reason alone, it is good for the singer to practice this sound.

Try singing the following words in 3/4 time. Sustain the first syllable for a half note and the second for a quarter note. Eventually, you should be able to sing the second syllable for the duration of a half note and the first, the shorter, quarter note.

Ro **ses**	whi **skers**	ki **ttens**	mi **ttens**
lo **ver**	mu si **cian**	mo **ther**	bro **ther**

Comparison

[I]				
big	bin	bid	Bic	bit
dip	did	dig	dill	dim
fit	fib	fig	fin	fish
giddy	gift	gig	gill	give
hid	hill	him	hip	hiss
kick	kid	kill	kin	kiss
lib	lick	lid	limo	lip
mid	mini	miss	mitt	mix
nick	nickel	nil	nip	knit
pig	pick	pill	pin	pimp
quick	equip	quill	quit	quiz
rib	rid	riff	rig	rim
sick	sill	simple	sin	sit
tick	till	tin	tip	tix
wick	widow	wig	will	win

[E]				
bed	beg	beck	bell	bend
debt	deck	dead	dell	den
fed	fell	February		
gel	guess	get		
head	heck	hell	hen	hex
keg	ketchup			
led	leg	ledge	less	
med	mega	men	mess	
neck	knell ("to ring")	next		
ped	peg	peck	pen	pet
question	quell			
red	wreck	wren	rep	
said	segue	sell	sent	
tech	teddy	tell	test	temp
web	wed	well	when	

Diction quiz

Which words have [æ] and which have [ʌ]?

[ ]
Lad
[ ]
Love
[ ]
Mad
[ ]
Mug
[ ]
Won
[ ]
Wag
[ ]
Glove
[ ]
Glad
[ ]
Above
[ ]
Bad
[ ]
Fan
[ ]
Club
[ ]
Clan
[ ]
Dumb
[ ]
Damn
[ ]
Fun

Comparison

[ɔ]		[ʌ]		[ɜ]
bomb	____________	bum	____________	burn
cop	____________	cup	____________	curl
wrong	____________	rung	____________	
dog	____________	dug	____________	**dir**ty
fawn	____________	fun	____________	first
jog	____________	jug	____________	germ
lost	____________	lust	____________	learn
Mom	____________	mum	____________	mirth
mod	____________	mud	____________	**mur**der
pop	____________	pup	____________	**pur**pose
stock	____________	stuck	____________	stern
talk	____________	tuck	____________	turn
long	____________	lung	____________	learn
gone	____________	gun	____________	girl
hot	____________	hut	____________	hurt
Ron	____________	run	____________	

Comparison of All Vowels

	[a]	[E]	[æ]	[ɔ]	[U]	[u]	[I]	[i]	[ʌ]	[ɜ]
b	bar	bed	bad	Bob	book	boo	bit	bee	bug	bird
d	dark	den	dad	dog	---	do	dip	deep	dumb	dirt
f	fa	fed	fad	fog	foot	fool	fill	feel	fun	first
h	ha	head	had	hot	hood	who	hit	heat	hug	her
j	jar	jello	jam	job	---	June	Jill	jean	jug	jerk
l	la	led	lad	log	look	loot	lip	leap	love	learn
m	ma	met	mad	mob	---	moo	mix	me	mug	murder
n	na	neck	nap	knob	nook	new	nick	knee	none	nerd
p	pa	pen	pad	pot	put	pool	pin	pea	pun	pearl

Differences from the Dictionary for Singers

1. **Syllabification.** The dictionary will syllabify words according to roots, prefixes and suffixes, double letters, etc., whereas singers will end each syllable with a vowel if possible.

2. **Diphthongs** should be written with open vowels. Example: Singers should write [E:i] and [ɔ :i], although you will see these written in the dictionary as [e:i] and [o:i]. *[e] and [o] don't exist in sung English, so using them in diphthongs would be confusing.

3. The dictionary will use [ɒ] rather than [ɔ] in some words. Although [ɒ] is used in spoken English, it is not used in singing. (See footnote for Madeleine Marshall's English Diction for Singers)

4. The dictionary will use IPA spellings that include the letter "r." Singers only pronounce "r" when it precedes a vowel.

5. The dictionary will use a colon ":" after some vowel sounds, indicating that they are to be sustained. Since our music determines how long we sustain each vowel, we don't need the colon.

6. The dictionary will not surround IPA symbols in **square brackets**; we will. Example: [i]

7. Dictionaries consider some one syllable words unstressed and thus use the **neutral symbol** [ə]; whereas in singing since all words receive **some** stress, we'll write the sound as [ɜ]. The sound is the same.

8. Vowels are often followed by [j], the letter "y" or [w], but since we want to keep vowels "open" for singing, we'll omit these sounds.

DIPHTHONGS

Diphthongs

There are 5.

The word "diphthong" (pronounced "d**i**f-thong" not "d**ip**-thong") comes from Greek; "di" meaning twice and "phthongos" meaning sound. So, a diphthong is sound composed of two vowels in succession in the same syllable.

1. [a:i]

Sustain the 1st of each vowel pair for the duration of the note you're singing. The 2nd vowel is pronounced **at the last second**, like turning off a light as you exit a room.

starting position

[a]

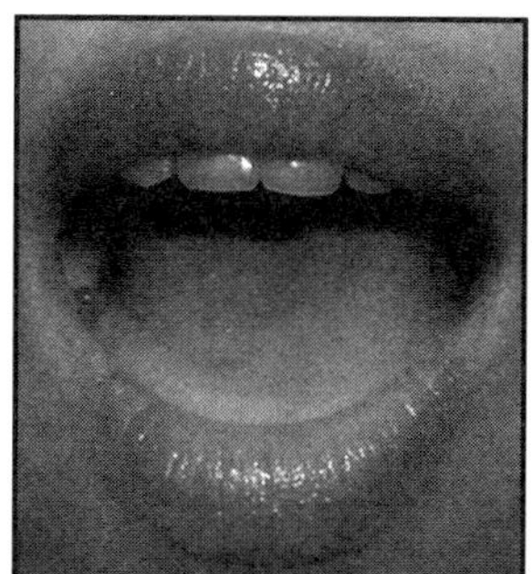

ending position

[i]

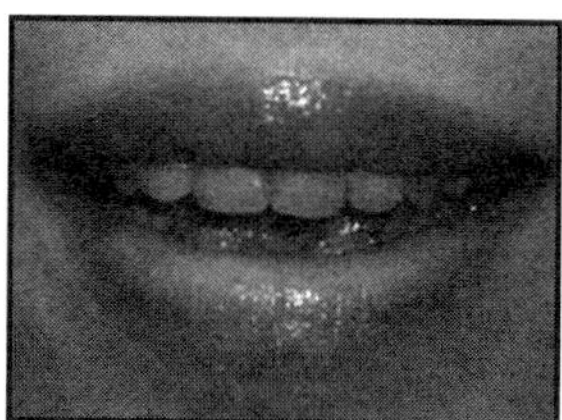

IMPORTANT: To correctly sing all diphthongs begin with the mouth position for the 1st vowel and smoothly sing through the 2nd vowel. The 1st vowel should be held almost for the entire note value, singing the 2nd vowel right right before the end of the note.
Sing each line below, holding the words with [a:i] for 4 beats.

1. You've got the **right** to **fight** for a **light**.
2. The **wine** is **fine** because it's **mine**.
3. **Smile** a **while**. It's the **style**.
4. The **pie** in the **sky** is too **high**.
5. Who will **buy** my **lie**?
6. **Why** are you sad? Did someone **die**?
7. Don't **cry**, it's just a **guy**. Say good**bye**.
8. **Hi, why** are you so **shy**?
9. I'm going to **buy** a **tie** for a **guy**.

[fl] and **[fr]** combinations are easily pronounced if you put your mouth in position to say the word only with the second consonant, [l] or [r], then, add the [f] by simply closing your lips. Let's do this together.

* For "fly" say "lie" then add the [f] in front.
* For "fry" say "rye" then add the [f] in front.

Consonants preceding [l] and [r]

Do the same as above

* Cry [kra:i]
* Try [tra:i]
* Dry [dra:i]
* Pry [pra:i]

-Ply [pla:i]
-Sly [sla:i]
-Fly [fla:i]

2 [E:i]

Sustain [E] adding [i] at the last instant

Start with [E]

End with [i]

Sing the lines below, sustaining **[E:i]**

1. **Hey**, that's good **bait**!
2. Please **save** the **date**.
3. Will the **gray** dog **stay away**?
4. The **game** is to **blame** for your **fame**.
5. **Wait** for your **date** when you get to the **gate**.
6. The **rain** in **Spain** stays **main**ly in the **plain**.
7. To **take** a **flake** isn't **fake**.
8. Don't **break** the **cake** until you **wake**.
9. You **came**; you **stayed**; the **flame** went out.

3. [ɔ:i]

begin with [ɔ]

end with [i]

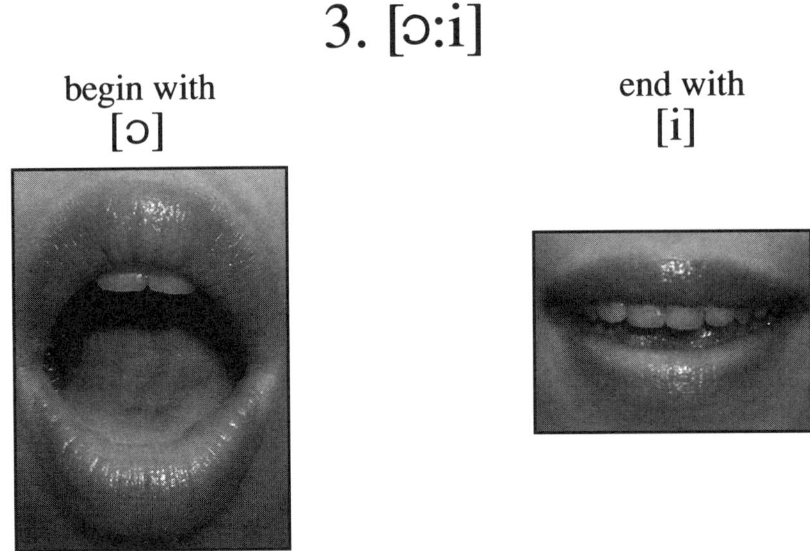

Sing these lines, **sustaining the first vowel** in the diphthong

1. I've found **joy**; I'm as happy as a baby **boy**
2. With a brand new choo choo **toy**
3. Re**joice**, re**joice** greatly
4. It's my **choice**; it's my **voice**.
5. You use **foil** to wrap gifts; but you **boil** potatoes that grew in **soil**
6. **Hoist** the sails; they're still **moist**
7. My **choice** is a **voice**
8. **Boys** will be **boys**

4. [a:u]

begin with [a] — end with [u]

Again, sing each line, sustaining bold syllables 4 beats

1. You're **bound** to wear a **crown** if you stay ar**ound**
2. You can't **drown** if you stay on dry **ground**.
3. He's nothin' but a **hound** dog.
4. I'll have a **pound** of **ground round**.
5. I **found floun**der at the grocery store.
6. **How now brown cow?**
7. The **bow-wow** needs a **tow**el for his **jowls**.
8. Our **town's** a **brown town**.
9. Get **out** you **lout**. I'm tired of your **pout**
10. Rock a bye little **hound down** on the **ground**.
11. Send in the **clowns**, there ought to be **clowns**
12. Don't get ar**ound** this **town** anymore.

5. [ɔ:u]

start with [ɔ] — end with [u]

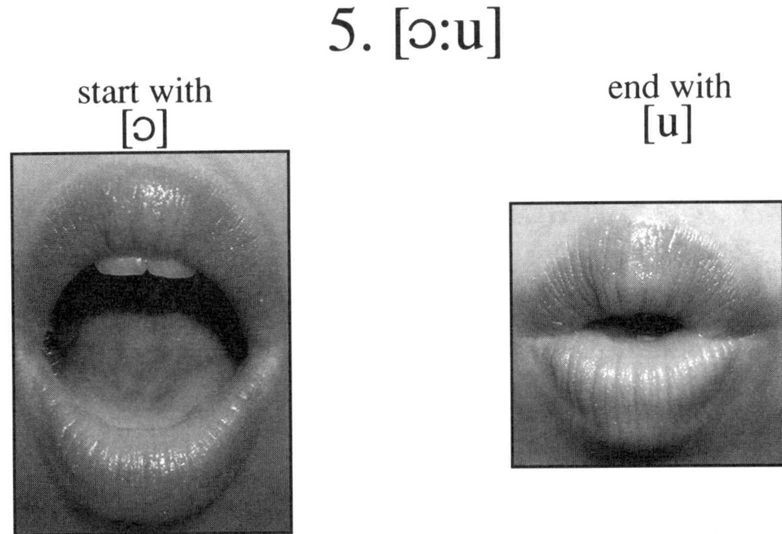

Now, sing the lines below, sustaining the first vowel in [ɔ:u]

1. I'll **go** to the **show** even if it **snows**
2. **Glow**, little **glow**-worm there's no **crow** around
3. Friend or **foe**, it's "on with the **show**".
4. "**No go**" said **Bozo**.
5. She's a real "**pro**"; she always knows if it's **so**.
6. When he's **grown**, he'll **know** you're **alone**.
7. Is it a **stone** or a **phone**? Neither, it's a **bone**.
8. Have you met Mr. **Jones**? Someone said that he's a **clone**.
9. Why is the car so slow?
10. Row row row your boat.

Diphthong Review

1. [a:i]

hi my eye skies die five

2. [E:i]

face name pay great fame bait

3. [ɔ:i]

boy join foil moist toy oil

4. [a:u]

now town bow proud cloud wow

5. [ɔ:u]

no phone road low so oat

Comparison of English Diphthongs (with all consonants preceding each)

[a:i]	[E:i]	[ɔ:i]	[a:u]	[ɔ:u]
bye	bay	boy	bough	beau
cry	crayon	coy	cow	cold
die	day	doily	down	doe
fine	feign	foil	found	foe
guy	gay	goy	gown	go
hi	hey	ahoy	how	hoe
——	jay	joy	jowl	Joe
kind	kay	coil	cow	Kona
life	lay	loyal	loud	loan
my	may	moist	Mau mau	moan
nite	nay	noise	now	no
pie	pay	poise	pow	pose
sight	say	soy	sound	sew
tie	take	toil	town	toe
vie	vain	voice	vow	vote
why	way	——	wow	woe
——	yay	——	yow	yo

American Diction Checkup

Now that you've completed the Vowels and Diphthongs
Let's see what you can recall - FROM MEMORY!

List the 5 open vowels:

1)

2)

3)

4)

5)

List the 2 closed vowels:

1)

2)

List the other 4 English Vowels:

1)

2)

3)

4)

List the 5 diphthongs:

1)

2)

3)

4)

5)

Below, circle all "r's" which would be pronounced; cross out silent ones and indicate when the "r" would be pronounced with the next word by using a connecting arrow.

1. star
2. far
3. Earth
4. hark
5. green
6. Cry
7. far away
8. sorrow

CONSONANTS

Consonant Differences from Classical Singing

1. Don't you [dɔːuntju] = becomes dontcha [dɔːuntʃʌ]

*remember the vowels are more important than the consonants- thus slightly louder

2. In English, double consonants are spoken and sung as singles

"Ladder" becomes [læ də]

"Summer" becomes [sʌ mə]

*This is different from Italian, where the 1st double consonant is imploded and the 2nd exploded.

3. Internal "t's" are either sounded as "d's" or are simply "imploded" rather than "exploded" and sung as a glottal.

Examples: "kitten" [kI tən] becomes [ki ʔn] [ʔ = glottal sound]

"better" [bEtə] becomes bedder [bE də]

4. Final "ing" is often spoken and sung as "in"

Therefore "**nothing**"[nʌθ iŋ] becomes "**nothin**" [nʌ θIn]

"**something**" [sʌm θiŋ] becomes "**somethin**" [sʌm θIn]

5. Some words are pronounced as they would be in casual American or slang:

"Because" is often written 'cuz by songwriters and pronounced [kʌ**z**]

6. Again, "r" is pronounced only when it is followed by a vowel.

American English Consonants

Alphabet	IPA symbol	"sample word"
Soft c	[s]	face
Hard c	[k]	cane
ch	[tʃ]	chip
d	[d]	dog
f	[f]	fee
Soft g	[ʒ]	Asian
Hard g	[g]	God
h	[h]	hose
j	[dʒ]	joy
k	[k]	bake
l	[l]	laugh
m	[m]	monkey/mama
n	[n]	new
p	[p]	puppy
q	[kw]	quick
r	[r]	red
unvoiced "s"	[s]	sew
voiced "s"	[z]	has
sh	[ʃ]	she
t	[t]	tiger
unvoiced th	[θ]	bath
voiced th	[ð]	these
w	[w]	wood
x	[ks]	fix
y	[j]	yes
z	[z]	zoom

How to Work on the Consonants section

You will need to practice speaking, then singing each of the consonant sounds until you can do them comfortably. Notice that example words sometimes give the sound at the beginning AND sometimes at the end. Ideally, you should sing each vowel sound with **each consonant** BOTH at the beginning and the end.
Example 1:

[u]

[bub] [dud] [fuf] [gug] etc.

Now sing phrases of your choice song, using only one consonant at a time.

Example 2: If you are working on the sound [l], begin and end each phrase with the sound [l].

"Happy Birthday to You" would become "la la la la la lal"

Tape record yourself until you sound comfortable on each consonant.

Finally, record yourself singing actual lyrics to a song and listen to whether any sounds indistinct or tense. If so, slow the tempo and try again.

Although we sing on vowels, consonants must be short, clean and sung with the same clarity and ease with which we produce the vowels; otherwise our legato will be lost.

Practice singing ballads in the style of your choice. The slow tempos will give you time to think of the appropriate sounds without your having to rush. *Remember, the singer sounds comfortable IF NEVER RUSHED. That includes singing on faster tempo songs also!

Consonant Schedule

I

[s]	soft c	"face"		
[k]	hard c	"cane, cake"		
[ʃ]	sh	"ship"		
[tʃ]	ch	"church, chip"		
[d]		"dud" "dude"		
[f]		"fee, fluff"		
[l]		"lull, lullaby"		
[r]		"red" "grrr"		

II

[ʒ]	soft g	"Asian" "beige"		
[g]	hard g	"God" "dog"		
[h]		"haha" "hoho"		
[dʒ]	"j"	"joy" "George"		
[k]		"kick"		
[m]		"mom"		
[n]		"none"	[ŋ]	so<u>ng</u>
[p]		"puppy" "pimp"		

III

[kw]	"q"	"quick"		
[s]	"soft s"	"sis"		
[z]	"hard s"	"has" "zazu";	[t]	"tot" "tight"
[θ]	soft th	"thin" "bath"		
[ð]	hard th	"this" "bathe"		
[v]		"viva" "verve";	[w]	"wow" "wawa"
[ks]	"x"	"fix"		
[j]	"y"	"yo" "yes" ;	[z]	"zoom" "lazy"

Comparison of [r] and [l]

Remember that in singing, "r" is only pronounced when before a sounded vowel!

[r]	[l]
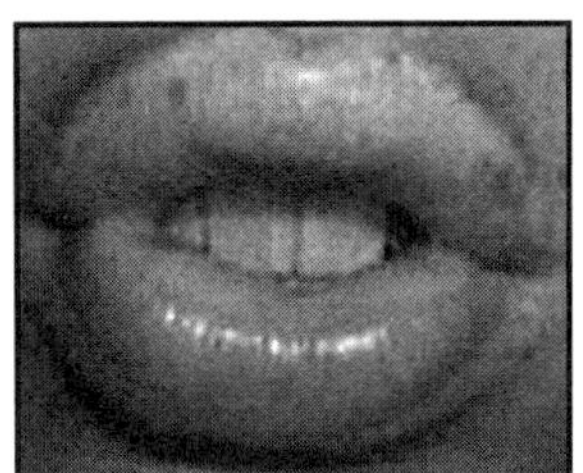	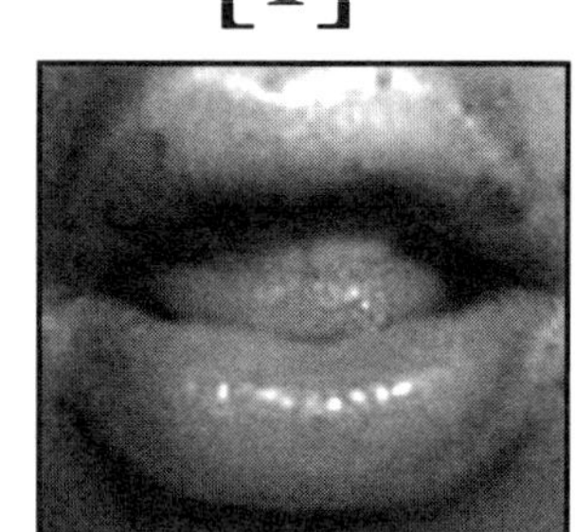
1. Mom gave her a **r**ed d**r**ess.	He **l**ed the **l**eague.
2. **R**ob's favorite music is **r**ock.	Did you **l**ock it?
3. His **r**obe is **r**eally **r**ed.	You're gonna **l**ose that gir**l**.
4. Here comes the **r**ail**r**oad car.	They rea**ll**y **l**oad on the work.
5. Is this **r**ye bread?	It's not a good habit to **l**ie.
6. Some singers don't eat dai**r**y.	They do practice dai**l**y!
7. That's the co**rr**ect answer.	Co**ll**ect the papers.
8. Do you see the fo**r**est or t**r**ees?	No more or **l**ess
9. I'm so so**rr**y.	Don't be si**ll**y.
10. We **r**ode in the ca**rr**iage.	That's quite a **l**oad!

Consonants I

		[s]	soft c	"face"		
sass	soft	see	said	say	sell	some
bass	boss	class	cost	fast	this	fist

	[k]	hard c	"cane, cake"		
cold	cough	coo	clown	come	cause
clue	croon	cow	cold	crown	call

	[ʃ]	sh	"ship"		
she	shine	show	should	share	shelf
wish	dish	fashion	gush	hush	lush

	[tʃ]	ch	"church, chip"		
chimp	chalice	choose	choice	cheap	chic
batch	match	catch	natural	pitch	rich

	[d]	"dud"	"dude"		
dark	day	deep	down	do	damp
bad	body	hid	mad	sadness	God

	[f]		"fee, fluff"		
friend	first	fine	flip	fizz	fan
calf	half	off	if	after	often

	[l]		"lull, lullaby"		
lips	lap	love	low	lay	lie

	[r]	"red"	"grrr"		
round	ran	wrap	rip	ray	run

Consonants II

[ʒ] and [ʃ]

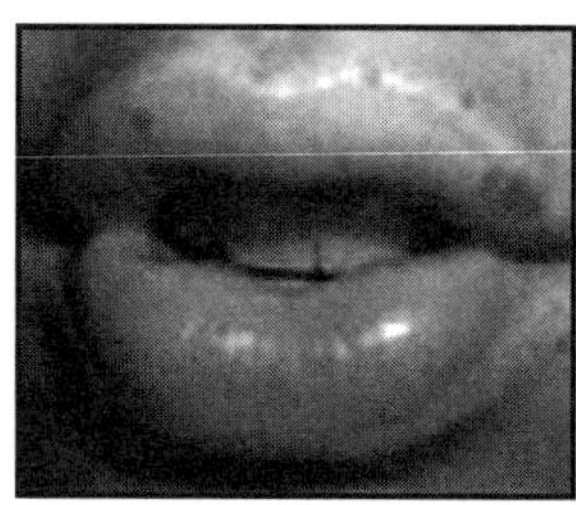

[ʒ] **soft g** mostly used in words borrowed from French such as "neige"

Asian	Asia	beige	bijoux	vision	visual	unusual

[dʒ]	**spelled as "j"or "g"**		**"joy"**		**"George"**
"orange"	joy	Joe	jump	jerk	jam
Jewish	jewelry	jammies	jumper	just	jar
Gem	gel	Jeff	sage	wedge	pudgy

[g]		**hard g**	**"God"**		**"dog"**
gig	go	gum	geek	get	gooey
beg	fog	mug	bag	egg	fig
green	glue	grass	grey	Greg	gone

	[h]	**"haha"**		**"hoho"**	
hip	hug	hey	hat	how	hi
HoHoHo	have	he	help	his	her
Hurt	happy	Herb vs.	herb	history	hello

		[k]		**"kick"**	
back	talk	dock	walk	stick	sock

[m] **"mom"**

home, "***mo***" ham, ***ma*** hem, ***men*** hum, ***must*** boom, ***mob***

[n] **"none"**

fine, ***knife*** fun, '***nuf*** man, "***Nam***" on, ***no*** goon, ***noogie***

[p] **"puppy" "pimp"**

lip,***pill*** rap, ***par*** dope, ***puddle*** hoop, ***Pooh*** kept, ***peck*** swept, ***pew***

Consonants III

[kw] **"q"** **"quick"**

quiet quell quad status quo quote quip
quit aqua equip equal quilt queen

[s] **"soft s"** **"sis"**

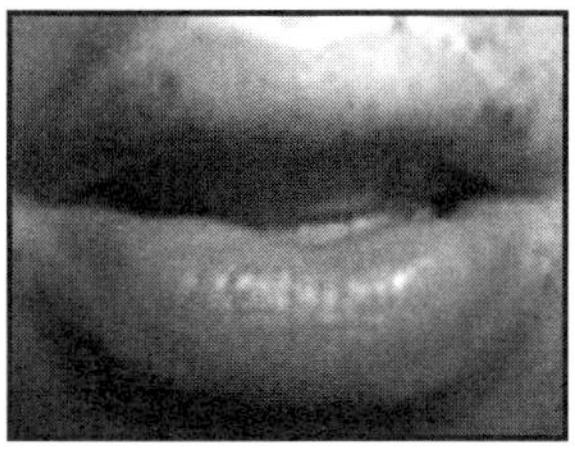

sip sift sister sea see saw sat
class brass sass hiss kiss miss dis

[z] **"hard s"** **"has"** **"zazu"**

zip fizz has because bees

[t] **"tot"** **"tight"**

tune time to top bat cat fat
fight right get yet set hit lit

[θ] **unvoiced th** **"thin"** **"bath"**

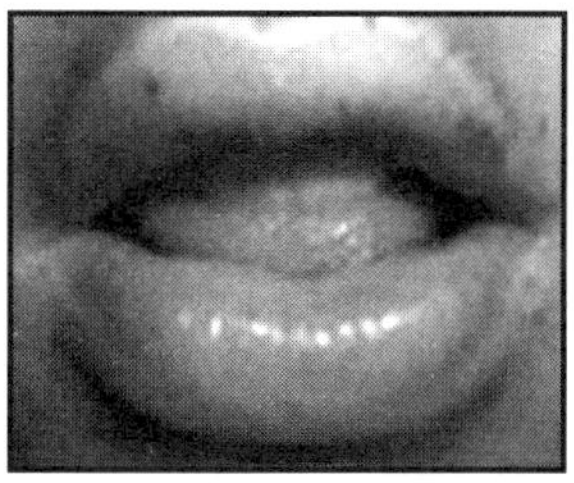

myth path death breath three both thick
through thanks thought three 'neath North

[ð] **voiced th** **"this"** **"bathe"**

breathe bother mother another them those they
thy thee these then tho'

[v] **"viva"** **"verve"**

voice vow valley voodoo save live love

		[w]	"wow"		"wawa"	
with	wife	wave	win	way	wow	we
few	lieu	how	now	wish	watch	will

		[ks]	"x"		"fix"	
mix	max	sax	foxy	fix	lax	packs

	[j]	"y"	"yo"	"yes"	
yet	you	yeah	year	yellow	your

	[z]	"zoom"		"lazy"	
zip	zoom	zig zag	zone	Zen	zany

"th" unvoiced [θ]

At word beginning:

thick
thin
think
three
thimble
thread
thought
thumb
throw
thirty
thank
thrill

At middle of word:

ether (gas)
mathematics

At end of word:

both
moth
math
mouth
south
bath
(pronounced with either American [æ]or British [a])

"th" voiced [ð]

At word beginning:

this
that
those
they
than
thee, thy, thou (Old English)
thus
them
the [ði] AND [ðʌ]

At middle of word:

usually before "ing"

At end of word:

bathe [bE:ið]
bother
either
neither, soothe
whether, weather
mother, father
lathe (tool)

Words which may be pronounced either way:

with, without

Consonant Combinations with "r"

		"breeze"
1. Say the word ending	-	[iz]
2. Say the word ending plus "r"	-	[riz]
3. Now say both consonants (ʃ)	-	[briz]

Some consonants which appear with "r"

BR	CR	DR	FR	GR	PR	TR
bring	crease	dream	free	green	preen	treat
broth	crawl	draw	frog	groggy	prod	trot
broom	croon	drool	fruit	group	proof	true
brittle	crib	drip	fritter	grip	prim	trip

Some consonants which appear with "l"

bleed	clean	fleet	glee	plea	sleep
blue	clue	flute	glue	plume	sloop
blame	clay	flame	glade	play	sleigh
blonde	clod	flop	glob	plod	slop
bland	clank	flan	gland	plant	slant
blip	clip	flip	glib	—	slip

Combinations with "th"

three throat thrust thread

Classwork on Consonants

Use each of the following consonants:
- **before** each vowel of the vowel triangle
- **after** each vowel
- **both** before and after

1. [r]
2. [l]
3. [ʃ]
4. [tʃ]
5. [θ]
6. [ð]

Problem: pronouncing "pr" and "pl" in "pray" and "play"
Solution: In order to easily pronounce consonants before "l" or "r," such as "p" form the mouth position for [l] or [r], then simply close your lips to form the [p]. That way you're ready to pronounce both!

Problem: pronouncing "thr" as in "three" or "through"
Similarly: With 3 consonants in a row as in "thr" or "three." "Th" is formed with the tongue between the teeth. (See picture page 47)
"R" is uvular with the lips slightly puckered; and "ee" only requires that the lips be drawn sideways. Practice one movement at a time until you can go smoothly through all 3.

Voiced and Unvoiced English Consonants

[t]/[d]
bet/bed

[p]/[b]
lip/lib

[f]/[v]
five (has both) life/lives

[k]/[g]
beak/beagle

[θ]/[ð]
"thin" "bath"/"this" "with"

[s]/[z]
size (has both) house/houses

[ʃ]/[ʒ]
Geisha/beige

~~~~~~

* [m] and [n]
*both are "voiced" but [m] is created by gently closing the lips, whereas [n] is created by touching the sides of the tongue to the upper gum ridge

[ch]/[dʒ]
church/George
~~~~~~

APPENDIX

How To Sing American CD

This recording is for students of *How to Sing American*. It includes all the American vowel and consonant sounds as appear in the International Phonetic Alphabet or IPA. It is necessary that you memorize the sound of each vowel so that you can picture it exactly .

Consulting the vowel triangle, we begin with the upper right corner and travel around the triangle, ending with the upper left corner. Next will come the two symbols in the center of the triangle and last, the 5 diphthongs used in English singing.

You may use this CD to improve your American English pronunciation by copying the sound of each vowel or, only those on which you need practice. Eventually you should be able to maintain each vowel sound for an entire melody.

Part I
American English Vowels

Each vowel will be started with an "h" sound so as to remove the possibility of any glottal interference or glottal attack. You will hear the name of the vowel/symbol, a sample word in English, the vowel on a single note, and finally, the same sound on a 5 note scale:

1. [u] "who"
2. [U] "hood"
3. [ɔ] "hot"
4. [ʌ] "hug" (this symbol may appear as an inverted "v" or a triangle)
5. [a] "fa" (be sure to keep this sound 'bright')
6. [æ] "have"
7. [E] "head"
8. [I] "hit
9. [i] "heat"

Now, to the center of the vowel triangle:

10.[ɜ] "heard" Since this sound is more difficult to explain than the others, please refer to the sound the Beatles used when they sang the word "girl." This symbol is a "reverse Epsilon;" we'll call it a "3". Note. It always appears in stressed syllables. Notice also that there is no following "r."
11.[ə] "the neutral" Similar in sound to the previous sound, but appearing in unstressed syllables only. An example of its use would be the 2nd syllable of the word "roses."

The 5 diphthongs

Each diphthong will be spelled out by its sounds (obtained from the previous vowels covered) and then given by an English word example first sung on a sustained note; then sung on a scale passage.

*Notice that moving lines occur on the 1st of the 2 vowels.

4. [a:i] "night"

5. [E:i] "day"

6. [ɔ:i] "boy"

7. [a:u] "now"

8. [ɔ:u] "no"
*Note that there is no closed "o" in English. This diphthong substitutes for that sound.

Part I
American English Consonants

Alphabet	IPA Symbol	"Sample Word"
Soft c	[s]	face
Hard c	[k]	cane
ch	[tʃ]	chip
d	[d]	dog
f	[f]	fee
Soft g	[ʒ]	Asian
Hard g	[g]	God
h	[h]	hose
j	[dʒ]	joy
k	[k]	bake
l	[l]	laugh
m	[m]	monkey/mama
n	[n]	new
p	[p]	puppy
q	[kw]	quick
r	[r]	red
unvoiced "s"	[s]	sew
voiced "s"	[z]	has
sh	[ʃ]	she
t	[t]	tiger
unvoiced th	[θ]	bath
voiced th	[ð]	these
w	[w]	wood
x	[ks]	fix
y	[j]	yes
z	[z]	zoom

Song Lyrics in IPA
Beautiful Dreamer

by Stephen Foster

[u] [ə] [ə] [i] [ə] [E:i] [ʌ] [u] [i]
Beau/ti/ful Drea/mer wake u/nto me,

[a] [a:i] [æ] [u] [ɔ] [a] [E:i] [i]
Sta/rlight and dew/drops are wai/ting

[ɔ] [i] [a:u] [ʌ] [ʌ] [u] [ɜ]
for thee. Sounds of the rude world

[ɜ] [I] [ʌ] [E:i] [ʌ] [a:i] [u]
heard in the day. Lulled by moon

[a:i] [æ] [ɔ] [æ] [ʌ] [E:i]
light have all passed a/way

Note that all steps from page 8 were completed.

1. Silent e's were crossed out.
2. Silent r's were crossed out.
3. Syllabification was done, and
4. the IPA vowel sounds were written in.

Here's line 1 of verse 2 with consonant IPA also:

[bju tə fəl] [dri mə] [kwi nʌv ma:i sɔŋ]
Beau/ti/ful drea/mer, queen of my song

Mystery Song

This song lyric is written entirely in IPA symbols.
Can you figure it out?

[dæ ʃiŋ θru ðʌ snɔ:u I nʌ wʌn hɔ sɔ:u pə

nslE:i. ɔ ðʌ fi ldzwi gɔ:u læ fi ŋɔ lðʌ wE:i.

bE lzɔ nbɔ btE:i lzriŋ mE:i kiŋ spI rI

tsbra:it. ɔ:u wʌt fʌ n I tI ztu si ŋʌ slE:i iŋ

sɔŋ tu na:it.]

[dʒiŋ əl bɛlz, dʒiŋəl bɛlz, dʒiŋəl ɔl ðʌ

[wE:i. ɔ:u wʌt fʌ nɪ tɪ ztu ra:i dɪ nʌ

wʌ nhɔ sɔ:u pə nslE:i]

Public Domain

IPA Fonts

This IPA font is available from the International Phonetic Society.

"sil manuscript"

qwertyuiop asdfghjklm zxcvbnm,.	lower case
æʷɛɾθʏʊɪø ɑʃð̌ɣɢʰ ʲʜɮʟ' ʒχð̌ʊβŋɱ,./	caps
ɜəɹʎʉɨœʢ ɒʂɤɠɦʄʡɫᵐɟ ʐ ɔʌɓɳɯɴˤ—	option

The International Phonetic Association exists to promote the study of the science of phonetics and the applications of that science. The Association can trace its history back to 1886, and since that time the most widely known aspect of its work has been the International Phonetic Alphabet.[2]

[2] Handbook of the International Phonetic Association (c) 1999 Cambridge University Press

Answers to Diction Quiz p. 27

[æ]
Lad
[ʌ]
Love
[æ]
Mad
[ʌ]
Mug
[ʌ]
Won
[æ]
Wag
[ʌ]
Glove
[æ]
Glad
[ʌ]
Above
[æ]
Bad
[æ]
fan
[ʌ]
Club
[æ]
clan
[ʌ]
dumb
[æ]
damn
[ʌ]
fun

Answers to American Diction Checkup p.36

List the 5 open vowels: a E I ɔ U

List the 2 closed vowels: ___i____ _____u_____

List the other 4 English Vowels: ɜ, ə,æ ,ʌ

List the 5 diphthongs: a:i, ɔ:i, E:i, a:u, ɔ:u

Below, circle all "r's" which would be pronounced; cross out silent ones and indicate when the "r" would be pronounced with the next word by using a connecting arrow.

1. sta~~r~~ 2. fa~~r~~

3. Ea~~r~~th 4. ha~~r~~k

5. green 6. Cry

7. far away 8. sorrow